SCOOB!

A DOG'S BEST FRIEND

based on the feature film *SCOOB!*

adapted by Tex Huntley

story by Matt Lieberman
and Eyal Podell & Jonathon E. Stewart

screenplay by Adam Sztykiel and Jack C. Donaldson
& Derek Elliott and Matt Lieberman

based on characters created by Hanna-Barbera Productions

illustrated by Day6

Random House 🏠 New York

Shaggy is
at the beach.
He is lonely.

Time for a picnic.
Shaggy has food.
But he has no
friends to eat with.

Shaggy makes
some friends
out of sand.

They are no fun.
They cannot share
his giant sandwich.

Shaggy meets
a puppy.
The puppy is hungry!

The puppy likes

Shaggy's giant sandwich!

What is the puppy's name?
Shaggy sees a box
of Scooby Snacks.
He names the puppy
Scoob.

Shaggy and Scoob become friends.

Shaggy gives Scoob

a special collar.

On Halloween,
Shaggy and Scoob meet
Velma, Daphne, and Fred.
They like to solve
mysteries.

The friends grow up together.

They become a team
called Mystery Inc.

Their van is
the Mystery
Machine.

22

Shaggy and Scoob's adventures
are just beginning!